A BOOK ABOUT TELLING TIME

Around the Clock with Harriet

By Betsy and Giulio Maestro

CROWN PUBLISHERS INC., NEW YORK

Library of Congress Cataloging in Publication Data
Maestro, Betsy.
Around the clock with Harriet.
Summary: Depicts Harriet and her activities at each
hour of the day.
[1. Time—Fiction] I. Maestro, Giulio. II. Title.
PZ7.M267Ar 1984 [E] 83-7664
ISBN 0-517-55118-7

Grandma gave Harriet a new watch.
Now Harriet could tell time.

8:00 AM

When Harriet woke up the
next day, her watch
said **8 o'clock.**
It was morning.

9:00 AM

After Harriet dressed and made her bed, she sat down to eat her breakfast.
Her watch said **9 o'clock**.

10:00 AM

Harriet cleaned up the kitchen and then went out to play. It was **10 o'clock.**

11:00 AM

Her watch said **11 o'clock** when Harriet visited the library.

12:00 NOON

When Harriet had a peanut butter sandwich for lunch, her watch said **12 o'clock**. It was noon.

1:00 PM

Harriet was tired.
She went home for a nap.
It was **1 o'clock.**

2:00 PM

At **2 o'clock,** Harriet was on her way to Mouse's house. The summer sun was hot.

3:00 PM

Harriet and her friend
had milk and cookies
at **3 o'clock.**

4:00 PM

When her watch said
4 o'clock, Harriet
was shopping.

5:00 PM

Harriet was in her kitchen at **5 o'clock.**

6:00 PM

At **6 o'clock**, Harriet ate her dinner.
It was evening.

7:00 PM

After dinner, Harriet
cleaned up and then
sat down to read.
Her watch said **7 o'clock.**

8:00 PM

Harriet got ready for bed.
When she climbed in,
it was **8 o'clock.**

12:00
MIDNIGHT

1:00 AM

2:00 AM

11:00 PM

10:00 PM

That night, as she slept, Harriet's watch ticked away.

9:00 PM

3:00 AM

4:00 AM

5:00 AM

6:00 AM

7:00 AM

All the hours of the night went by,
until . . .

8:00 AM

at **8 o'clock** in the morning, Harriet began her new day.